Vila is a small island in the South Pacific. A young man called Kaloris lived on Vila. He was very skilled with a bow. He spent much of his time practicing with his bow and arrows. He could shoot an arrow further and straighter than anyone else on the island.

One evening when he had been practicing with his bow and arrow, he decided to go for a swim in the sea. He put his bow and his quiver of arrows down on the sand and waded into the waves. He swam for a bit and then floated on his back and looked up at the twinkling stars in the sky.

Then he looked at the big silver Moon shining in the night sky. He could see patterns and shapes on the surface of the Moon and he started to think about what it was like on the Moon.

He swam back to the shore and walked to where he had left his bow and arrows.

He picked up his bow and an arrow and looked up at the Moon. He took careful aim, and then shot at the Moon. The arrow flew straight up, hit the surface of the Moon, and stayed there. Kaloris smiled and took another arrow.

He aimed at the Moon again, and shot a second arrow. This arrow also flew straight up to the Moon, but this time it struck the first arrow and got stuck in it. Kaloris continued to fire arrows at the Moon. Each arrow got stuck in the one before until he had a line of arrows stretching down from the Moon to the beach where he stood.

Kaloris picked up his bow and quiver of arrows and slung it over his back. He then started to climb up the line of arrows. At last, he reached the Moon. He looked around himself at the rocks and the silver dust. Then he was very surprised to see a large trapdoor just to his left.

He walked across to the trapdoor and looked at it. It was difficult to see, which is why he could not see it from the beach. Then he walked all around it. He could see a big metal ring attached to it. He picked up the ring, knocked firmly on the door and waited.

"Come in," called a deep voice.

Kaloris took hold of the ring and turned the door handle. He opened the door and peered into the Moon. It was dark inside but he could just see a man, sitting at a table and eating. Kaloris stepped inside and greeted the man in the Moon politely.

He explained how he had seen the Moon and had seen the shapes and patterns on its surface, and had decided to visit it. He told the man in the Moon how he had shot a line of arrows and climbed up it.

The food the man in the Moon was eating smelled lovely. Kaloris became aware that he was very hungry, and that he had not had dinner before climbing up to the Moon. His tummy rumbled and the man in the Moon chuckled.

“You are hungry,” he said. “Please have some food.”

He spooned out a big bowl of what he was eating and offered it to him. Kaloris took the dish and started eating. It tasted amazing.

“I have never eaten anything so good,” he told the man in the Moon, as he scraped his bowl and finished it all up.

"What is this strange vegetable?" Kaloris wanted to know.

"These are called yams," said the man in the Moon. "Do you not have yams on the island where you live?"

Kaloris shook his head, "No," he said. "I have never eaten or seen anything like it."

The man in the Moon explained how to grow and cook yams.

“I don’t often have visitors,” said the man in the Moon. “It is nice to see someone and to chat about what is happening below. As you have taken the time to come and visit and speak to me, I am going to give you and your island a present of some yams.”

With that he stood up and fetched a sack of yams. He opened the trapdoor and threw all of the yams out. The yams tumbled away from the Moon, down into the clouds and then continued on, raining down to the ground. They landed and bounced all over the beach at the bottom of the line of arrows.

Kaloris thanked the man in the Moon. He told him that everyone on the island would love the yams. He followed the yams out of the door and carefully closed it, turning the handle to shut it. When he turned back to look at it again the trapdoor had vanished. Kaloris shook his head and then started the long climb back down to the beach.

The islanders were very pleased when Kaloris showed them the yams. He showed them how to put them in the ground and give them lots to drink. When the yams had grown, he showed them how to cook them. From then on, every time they ate yams they remembered Kaloris, his skill with a bow and arrow, and his visit to the man in the Moon!